DELLA REESE

God Inside of Me

Illustrated by Yvonne Buchanan

Jump at the Sun
Hyperion Books for Children
New York

There was only one thing Kenisha didn't like about going to Sunday school. And that was that she had to take her little brother, Eli, along.

Eli wasn't a bad kid. Eli wasn't a pest. But Eli walked too slow for Kenisha.

Kenisha hated to be late for church. She was sure that if Eli kept walking so slow, they'd miss the first Sunday school lesson.

Each time they walked to church, Eli stopped to stare at everything—the butterflies, the squirrels, the crooked-neck tree.

This Sunday was no different. Kenisha had to keep telling Eli, "Hurry it up a little, will ya?"

Like every other Sunday, once Kenisha got to Sunday school everything was fine, and Kenisha started feeling good inside.

There were the Bible stories Mrs. Allswell told—and she told them so smooth. And there was the way the children got to recite the Bible verses they'd been learning at home all week.

And there was the singing—ooh, the sweet singing! There was singing before Mrs. Allswell told a smooth story. There was singing after the story was through. And there was singing between the Bible verses.

Sunday school was so much fun.

As Kenisha and Eli left church that Sunday, Kenisha was still singing the last song they sang in Sunday school. It was a new song, and Kenisha wanted to sing it all the way home—and then sing it some more. But Kenisha had to keep stopping her song to tell Eli, "That's the same tree you saw this morning. It's the same tree you see *every* Sunday on the way to church and on the way back home."

"I know, Neesha," said Eli. "But — "

"Then you ought to know there's nothing new to see," interrupted Kenisha. "And if you keep dawdling and staring at things," she warned, "you'll wear out your eyeballs!" Kenisha didn't think she could take another Sunday like this.

Eli wondered if maybe Kenisha was right about how staring could wear out your eyeballs. Just in case she was right, he figured maybe he'd save up all his staring for next week when they'd walk past this same tree again. For now, he'd just let his eyes roam a little. Then he started walking a bit faster so Kenisha wouldn't get more angry.

Kenisha started up again with her song. Her ponytail was swinging. Eli started skipping along.

That's when Kenisha spotted Rabunny and stopped her song for good.

Rabunny was at it again, lying on the porch, fast asleep, snoring like a tired old train whistle! His sleeping and his *snore-whistle-snore* always sent Kenisha into a tizzy.

"You big-bellied bunny!" Kenisha called out as she raced to the porch. "Wake up, Rabunny, and stop that racket."

Rabunny was too asleep to hear Kenisha. His *snore-whistle-snore* bounced on the breeze.

Eli thought Rabunny's *snore-whistle-snore* was funny. He knew it made Kenisha mad, so he didn't say a word. But Eli was laughing inside as he held open the door and watched Kenisha pick up Rabunny and lug him into the house. As she did, she muttered, "Here I got me a new song I learned just this morning—a sweet song that ain't so sweet with a *snore-whistle-snore* thrown in!"

Eli ran up the stairs and into his room.

When Kenisha got to her bedroom door, she shook Rabunny.
"Now you stay in here where you belong," she said, "with
Rackeroon and her too-many questions, and Clown who can't
make up his mind about anything."

Dolly Dear greeted Kenisha and Rabunny at the door. Dolly
Dear was the mama of the bunch. She had more patience than
anybody. And she knew so much about so many things. Nobody
ruffled Dolly Dear. Not Rackeroon. Not Clown. Not even
Rabunny.

"I was just looking for Rabunny," Dolly Dear said. "Where's he been?"

"Rabunny's been sleeping on the porch, rattling creation with his *snore-whistle-snore*," said Kenisha. She rolled Rabunny into his basket by her bed, hoping to stir him from his sleep. But nothing could wake that critter. He just kept on sleeping, kept on *snoring*.

Dolly Dear could see that Kenisha was in one of her tizzies over Rabunny. She thought it best to change the subject.

"And how was your time at church?" Dolly Dear asked.

"It was wonderful, so wonderful," said Kenisha. "Singing, praying, feeling God's goodness from way deep down. But my feeling-fine time turns sour as soon as Rabunny starts up with his sleepyheaded self. How can a girl hold on to the peace of God when she comes home to a long-legged, long-eared, big-bellied bunny, snoring loud enough to shake the leaves from the trees?" And Kenisha wasn't finished. "On top of that, I had to walk with my slowpoke little brother!" Rabunny let out a snort and tumbled from his basket. He was still fast asleep, and on to a louder *snore-whistle-snore*.

"You see what I mean?" Kenisha said.

Dolly Dear smiled. "God teaches us peace through patience, child," she said, "and through finding the good in everyone, even those who get on our nerves. Why do you think God puts so many pain-in-the-neck things in our path?"

"But if Rabunny keeps it up, he'll sleep his life away," said Kenisha. "If I don't stop him, he'll—"

Before Kenisha could finish, up jumped Rackeroon with her
million questions. "And why do you think God made the water
blue? And how come birds got wings? And why do clouds
look like pillows in the sky?"

Kenisha folded her arms tight in front of her. She was trying to do what Dolly Dear said—find the good in everybody and if not the good, then at least the okay.

But it was hard.

First so-slow Eli. Then Rabunny's *snore-whistle-snore*. And now Rackeroon with her too-many questions!

"What makes mountains so tall?" she asked.

"Rackeroon!" Kenisha shouted. "You're going to give yourself a headache if you keep asking so many questions." Kenisha sat down on the corner of her bed. "Goodness!" she huffed.

From where Clown was sitting in the window seat it looked
to him as if Kenisha was about to cry.

It's true that most times Clown couldn't make up his mind
about how he felt about things, but right now he was certain
that he didn't want Kenisha to cry. "It's such a lovely morning!"
Clown hoped that would cheer up Kenisha.

Kenisha looked at Clown. Through the window she saw babbler birds playing tag in the tree. A tiny smile crossed her face. And Clown smiled when he saw that Kenisha wasn't going to cry.

Then he looked down at his feet. Clown still hadn't decided which shoes he'd wear today.

"Hmmm." Clown crossed his legs. "The red shoes make me happy . . . but so do the blue," he said. Then Clown uncrossed his legs. "What am I to do? The red ones . . . or the blue?"

Kenisha rolled her eyes. "Clown, you have to stop being so wishy-washy. You have to learn to make up your mind—just like I make up my bed."

Kenisha looked around the room and shook her head.

Clown was still murmuring, "The red ones . . . or the blue," and crisscrossing his legs.

"Why can't birds fly to the moon?" asked Rackeroon, who was still staring at the babbler birds outside.

All the while Rabunny was still doing his *snore-whistle-snore*.

Kenisha was in a big tizzy now. She didn't think she could take it anymore. "Oh, Lordy, give me strength!" she cried out. "How in the world will I ever fix up this wacky, batty bunch?"

For a slow minute, Dolly Dear just looked at Kenisha. Then, Dolly Dear said, "The thing that's got me stumped, Miss Kenisha, is why you go to that church school every Sunday when you don't believe what they say."

Kenisha blinked. "I *do* believe what I learn in Sunday school, Dolly Dear," she said.

"Well, you're not acting like you do." Dolly Dear sighed. "For one thing, the last time you took me to church I heard Mrs. Allswell say that everything and everybody comes into the world with everything they need inside of them. Do you remember that, Kenisha?"

Kenisha nodded.

"And do you also remember what Mrs. Allswell said about an apple, about how it has the color it would be and the kind of apple it would be and how it would taste, all in the seed?"

Kenisha nodded again. Then she whispered, "Everything and everybody has everything they need inside them . . ."

All of a sudden the room got quiet. There wasn't even the hint of a question in Rackeroon's eyes. Clown didn't look so befuddled. Not even a soft *snore-whistle-snore* came from Rabunny.

Kenisha brightened. "Dolly Dear, now I remember everything Mrs. Allswell said. She said that there is a piece of God in us, and inside that piece of God is all the stuff we need."

Rabunny leaned up and opened one eye. "What I need is to eat a whole field of carrots," he said with a yawn. Lazing back down, he asked, "Is that inside me?"

Dolly Dear could see Kenisha was about to fuss. "Child, don't get into another tizzy," Dolly Dear warned.

"But, Dolly Dear," said Kenisha, "Rabunny wants to eat a whole field of carrots—that makes no sense!"

"Kenisha, don't pay Rabunny no mind. Just let the piece of God in him take care of him. Rabunny can't eat a whole field of carrots anyway. At least not at one time."

Kenisha laughed. And then Dolly Dear laughed. And then Rackeroon and Clown laughed, too. Even Rabunny laughed, just before he looped back into a snooze and let loose a new *snore-whistle-snore*.

Kenisha felt a whole lot better. But there was one more thing she wanted to get clear with Dolly Dear.

"Are you saying that God wants Rabunny to be a sleepyhead?" asked Kenisha. "And that God wants Rackeroon to ask a million questions, and that Clown is supposed to have a two-way mind?"

Dolly Dear chuckled. "I don't have the tail end of a clue what God wants other folks to be or not. But I do believe that if

something needs fixing, the piece of God inside of them will take care of it."

Kenisha jumped up. She was sparkling inside, and it showed in her eyes. "I get it, Dolly Dear, I get it all. And I promise, I promise, I'll never let what Mrs. Allswell said slip from my mind!"

"That's right, honey!" cheered Dolly Dear. "Let go and let God."

Kenisha started singing the sweet song she'd learned that morning in Sunday school.

Clown did somersaults back and forth across the room. Rackeroon swished her whiskers to the tune.

As for Rabunny, he clapped and clapped his hands. But it wasn't long before he nestled back down in his basket—and you know what came next. That's right.

Snore-whistle-snore.

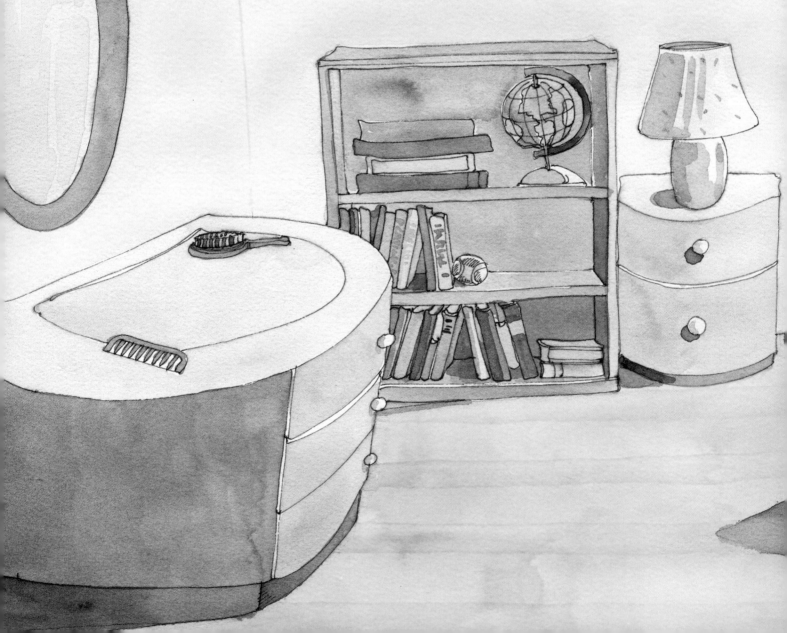

When the next Sunday came along, Kenisha left home singing last week's new song. And this Sunday she was taking everybody with her to church.

Under one arm Eli carried Clown, who had on one red shoe and one blue. Under Eli's other arm was Rackeroon, who asked Eli ten-times-ten questions about butterflies.

Kenisha carried Dolly Dear who was glad she'd be seeing Mrs. Allswell again. And Kenisha carried Rabunny whose *snore-whistle-snore* was bouncing on the breeze.

But today Rabunny's snore didn't send Kenisha into a tizzy. Neither did Rackeroon's questions. Or Clown's mix-matched shoes. She didn't worry about Eli growing up to be a lazybones even though he dawdled like always. And she didn't even worry that he'd wear out his eyeballs from staring at the crooked-neck tree.

Kenisha just kept stepping, singing all the way to church, and thinking maybe Mrs. Allswell would teach them another new song this week.

To my children and all of the children of the world
so that they will know for sure that there is a piece of God inside of them.
—D.R.

Printed in the United States of America.

FIRST EDITION
1 3 5 7 9 10 8 6 4 2

The artwork for this book was prepared using watercolor.
This book is set in .17/24-point Phaistos.

Library of Congress cataloging-in-publication data

Reese, Della.
God inside of me/Della Reese; illustrated by Yvonne Buchanan.
p. cm.
Summary: In dealing with her misbehaving, frustrating toys
and pondering what she has heard in Sunday School,
Kenisha realizes that there is a piece of God in each of us
and inside that piece of God is all the stuff we need.
ISBN 0-7868-0434-3 (hc).
[1. Christian life-Fiction. 2. Toys-Fiction. 3. Afro-Americans-Fiction.]
I. Buchanan, Yvonne, ill. II. Title.
PZ7.R25495Go 1999
[Fic]-dc21 98-45112